A Metaphor is a figure of speech, that is used to make a comparison between two things that aren't alike, but do have something in common.

Dedicated to Dylan James DePina, my prayer is that you will always be reminded by my voice to keep trying no matter how hard or how strange it feels. Focus on the process the product will always come.
Love,
Mama

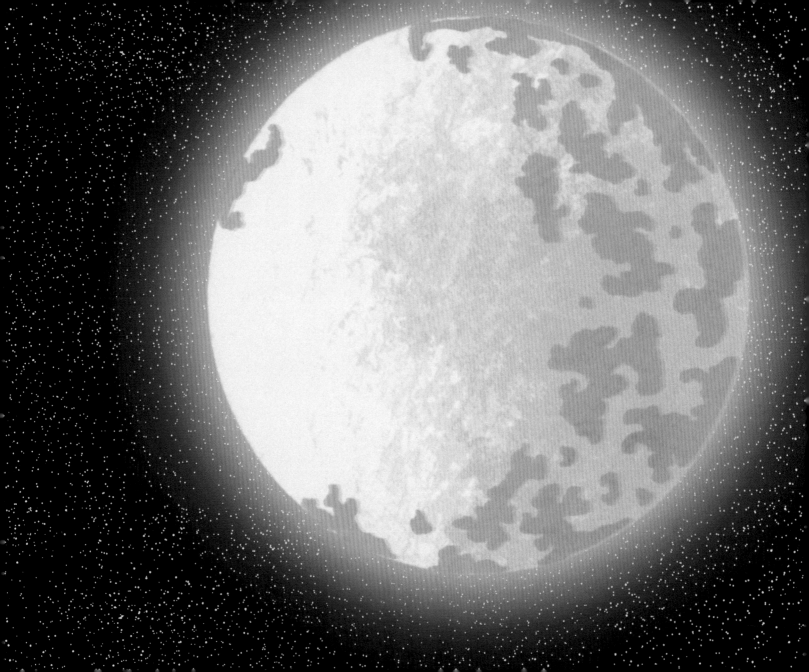

Why not?

It's sooo far away!

It is! But I can't let that stop me!

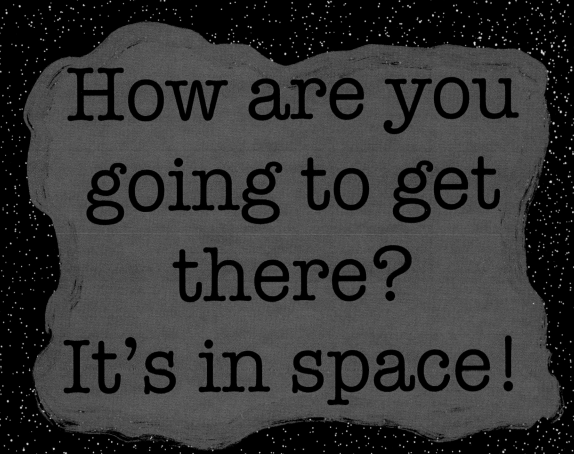

How are you
going to get
there?
It's in space!

I'm going to build a Rocket Ship!

But you don't know how.

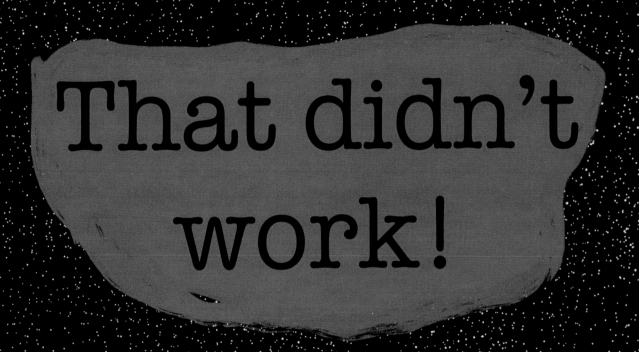

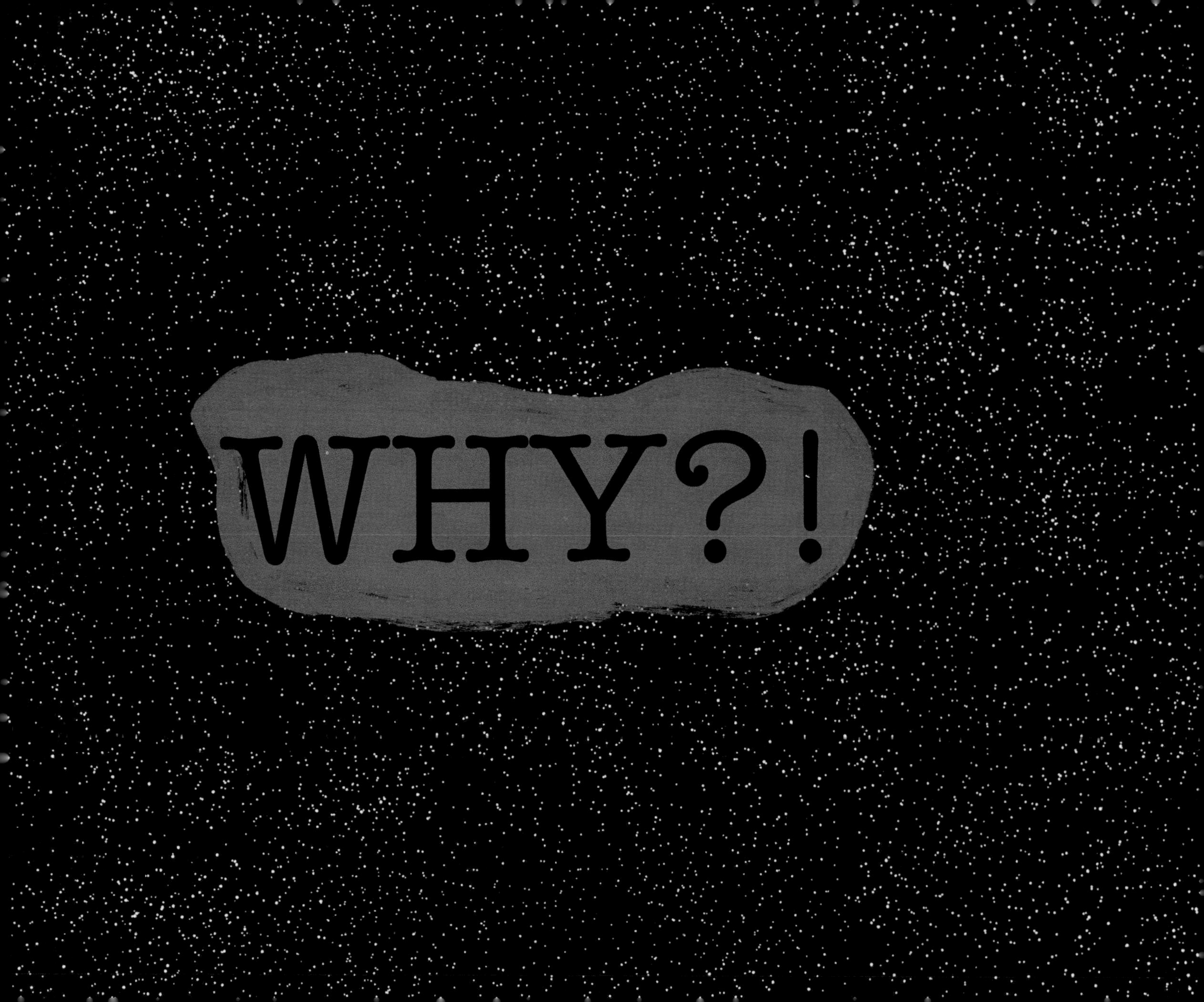
WHY?!

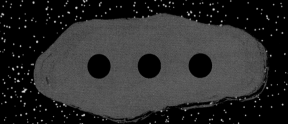

Mom says, that I have to learn from my mistakes and just build it stronger!

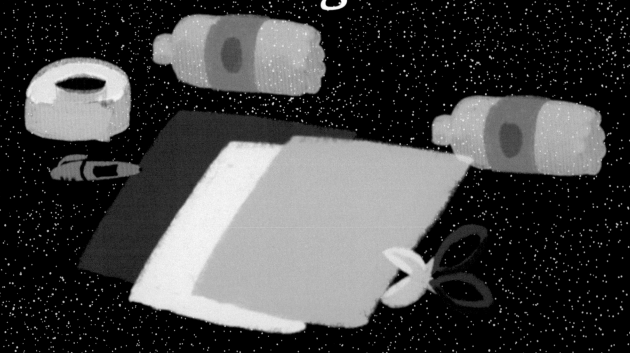

What if you still
can't do it?

Well now the sun is rising, The moon will disappear!

Just because we can't see it, doesn't mean that it's not still there.

Materials

* Cardboard boxes
* Tape
* Markers
* Crayons
* Glue
* Scissors
* Bottles
* Construction Paper
* Anything else you can find :)